To Bill, the best papa I know.
And to Georgia and Atticus,
who are so loved,
and were even "back in the egg."
—A.B.K.

For the love inside of you
that moves you to action
—C.O.

The artwork for this book was created with watercolor, ink, and mixed digital media.

Cataloging-in-Publication Data has been applied for and may be obtained from the Library of Congress.

ISBN 978-1-4197-4589-8

Text copyright © 2021 Angela Burke Kunkel
Illustrations copyright © 2021 Catherine Odell
Book design by Hana Anouk Nakamura

Printed and bound in China
10 9 8 7 6 5 4 3 2 1

For bulk discount inquiries, contact specialsales@abramsbooks.com.

ABRAMS The Art of Books
195 Broadway, New York, NY 10007
abramsbooks.com

Penguin Journey

written by ANGELA BURKE KUNKEL

illustrated by CATHERINE ODELL

ABRAMS APPLESEED

NEW YORK

Packed snow.

Moon glow.

Windblown.

All alone.

Empty view.

Now two!

Waves glitter.

Flippers flitter.

Fall in line,

journey time.

Sun, guide.

Ice, glide.

Partner, mate?

Rest, wait.

Journey through.

Mamas, too!

Swing, sway.

Call, play.

Beaks in air.

Now a pair.

Egg here,

keep near.

Feet kiss.   Near miss!

Croon goodbye,

touch, sigh.

Dark days.

Papa stays.

Mamas stand,

edge of land.

Into sea,

diving, free.

Left on land,

papas stand.

Baby wakes.

Egg breaks.

Mamas know

it's time to go.

Journey back

in starry black.

Two, now three,

face out to sea.

Snow glows.

Wind blows.

Day grows.

No matter the weather,

a family together.

AUTHOR'S NOTE

Emperor penguins are some of the most committed parents in the animal kingdom. Despite harsh conditions, both mother and father do their best to provide their chick with love and care. The process begins when male emperor penguins emerge from the sea in March or April, then travel to the interior of Antarctica, which ensures any offspring will be safe from the sea ice. After the female penguin produces an egg, it is immediately transferred to the father, who balances the egg between his feet and a special fold of skin to protect the developing chick from subzero temperatures. While the mother penguin must leave immediately in order to feed (and in order to provide nourishment for her chick), the father waits without food through the dark Antarctic winter. His only job is to keep the egg safe and warm.

While this story ends with male and female penguin reuniting and the mother meeting her chick for the first time, both parents share parenting duties for many more months. This includes several more rounds of each parent leaving to hunt for food, until the chick has molted—shed its baby feathers—and is old enough to enter the ocean and search for food on its own. Both parents do everything they can to ensure their chick's survival in the most extreme environment on Earth.

Sadly, breeding grounds for emperor penguins are shrinking due to climate change, and their population is in decline. Despite their brilliant adaptions, emperor penguins need our help. Hopefully, our human family will act to protect theirs.

SOURCES

Attenborough, David. *The Life of Birds*. BBC Books, 1998.

Borenstein, Seth. "Major Emperor Penguin Breeding Ground Gone Barren since 2016." Associated Press, April 24, 2019. See www.apnews.com/4629dfad58f540229b9bbae3b4581249.

Downer, John, director. *Snow Chick: A Penguin's Tale*. John Downer Productions/BBC, 2015.

"Emperor Penguin Breeding Cycle." Australian Government, Department of the Environment and Energy, Australian Antarctic Division, September 17, 2014. See www.antarctica.gov.au/about-antarctica/wildlife/animals/penguins/emperor-penguins/breeding-cycle.

Jacquet, Luc, director. *March of the Penguins*. Warner Independent Pictures, 2005.

———. *March of the Penguins 2: The Next Step*. Bonne Pioche/Disneynature, 2017.